Text copyright © 1991 Helen Muir
Illustrations copyright © 1991 Linda Birch

First published in Great Britain in 1991
by Simon & Schuster Young Books

Reprinted 1991

Photoset in 16pt Plantin by Goodfellow & Egan Ltd, Cambridge
Colour origination by Scantrans Pte Ltd, Singapore

Printed and bound in Belgium by
Proost International Book Production

Simon & Schuster Young Books
Simon & Schuster Ltd
Wolsey House
Wolsey Road
Hemel Hempstead HP2 4SS

BRITISH LIBRARY CATALOGUING IN PUBLICATION DATA
Muir, Helen
   Wonderwitch and the rooftop cats.
   I. Title   II. Birch, Linda   III. Series
   823.914 [J]

   ISBN 0-7500-0885-7
   ISBN 0-7500-0886-5 pbk

Wonderwitch
and the Rooftop Cats

Helen Muir

Illustrated by Linda Birch

SIMON & SCHUSTER

LONDON • SYDNEY • NEW YORK • TOKYO • SINGAPORE • TORONTO

For Hilary, Margaret and Jack

Cat Business

This witch was a Wonderwitch. She had a black cat and a tall hat and she thought she was a lot more important than ordinary witches.

She liked jokes and jelly babies but she also wanted to do something new and exciting every day.

At night, when it was growing dark, Wonderwitch and her black cat went for a ride together on her broomstick.

As they sailed over the trees and up over the tops of houses and flats, they could see the roof cats out on the tiles.

The cats came leaping from skylights, up fire escapes and out of attic windows.

In the moonlight they chased moths, chased each other or yowled. Mostly they sat, sniffing the night air, and stared into space.

There was ginger Sid, Shusha the Siamese, small black Jet, fat Jack, one-eyed Honeybun, saucer-eyed Flora, old boy Bruiser, Sweet Chebbs, torn-eared Leo and Poppet.

The black cat always made the witch stop.

"Cats!" she kept saying. "Oh how boring! If you're a Wonderwitch as I am you haven't time to hang about gawping at cats gawping at each other.

"I'm sick to death of cat calendars, cat books, cat this, cat that. There are far too many cats around for my liking."

While the black cat whispered into Bruiser's earhole, she sat on a chimney eating jelly babies and grumbling to herself.

Sometimes she mooched off looking for pigeons' eggs and peeped into bedroom windows at people sleeping with cats on their beds. Slowly a wonderful idea came into her mind.

"Witch Wotnot hasn't got a cat," she mused. "Neither has Witch Windbag. Every witch needs a witch's cat and there are a lot of witches."

"But does a cat need a witch?" the black cat sniffed.

"Shush!" Wonderwitch cackled, "I shall speak to Wotnot and Windbag. I might go into the cat-crazy industry myself!"

She called on Witch Wotnot who was doing the ironing in her snakeskin mini-skirt and diamond tiara.

"Call me a softie," Wotnot cooed, "I won't say no to a cuddly black fur ball to warm my feet on cold nights and save the heating bill."

Wonderwitch snapped her fingers. She knew where there was a black cat to be had for nothing. "One priceless witch's cat coming up! A bargain at a hundred quid!"

Next night on the rooftops, she got off her broomstick carrying a cat basket.

"Chi . . . chi . . . chi!" she called in a sugary voice to small black Jet.

The cats watched her. Jet waited till the witch was near enough to catch her then she sprang into a bathroom window and was gone.

Wonderwitch banged her nose and her hat fell off.

After that the
wicked old dame
became more
cunning. She landed
with a handful of
Mew Mew biscuits
and a mackerel
head. She hid
behind a chimney,
hooting like
an owl, and
waited.

Jet didn't come for the food. The other cats
did. When they had eaten everything in sight,
the witch lost her temper. Cursing loudly, she
climbed into the bathroom window of Jet's
house to find her.

In the dark, Wonderwitch bumped into
things and woke up Jet's owner. He hit her
three times with a golf club.

Witch Wotnot was getting annoyed. "Well, where's my cat then?" she demanded. "Get it or give my money back."

Wonderwitch spoke grandly, despite her black eye and bandaged arm. "My spell is nearly done. The cat will be yours by midnight."

But when she went back to the rooftop she could only grab torn-eared Leo. She was clawed to bits.

As the clock struck, Wotnot was waiting, dressed in black in honour of the new cat. When Wonderwitch produced a tabby-cat, she was extremely cross.

"This cat is not witch's black. Why is its ear torn?"

"My dear," Wonderwitch answered, quickly thinking of a way to please her, "this is one of the Great Fighting Cats, as old as time, magicked back from the court of Merlin. I thought you knew witches' cats were tabby in those days?"

The black cat choked.

"Take it or leave it," said Wonderwitch. "I have a waiting list for cats as long as my good arm."

Wotnot's friend, Witch Windbag, was very jealous when she heard about the tabby-cat.

"I want a Champion Fighting Cat, as old as time," Windbag demanded. "Can you work the same spell for me?"

"Difficult to do it twice although I am a Wonderwitch. I will need three thousand pounds." She knew she could never find another cat like Leo. She would have to try magic.

She shut herself up at home, muttering and mixing, while the worried black cat looked on.

"Dragon's eyes, giant's claws
Bullet head, killer jaws . . ."

Suddenly a thick yellow mist filled the kitchen and a fearsome fire-breathing creature crushed the washing machine, and cracked a wall, before Wonderwitch shrieked out some words and got rid of it.

The truth was, copying torn-eared Leo was beyond her powers. Exhausted, the witch went to bed and stayed there.

"Where's my cat, crook?" Witch Windbag banged on the door and shouted through the letter box, "I'm calling the police!"

This time Wonderwitch went back to the roof disguised as a gorse bush. But the only cat she managed to catch was ginger Sid. She sprinkled some sparkly stuff on his fur and took him round to Windbag.

Her voice rang out in a majestic manner. "Here is a cat from the palace bedchamber of King Henry VIII! Royal cats, as I expect you know, madam, were always ginger in the Middle Ages."

"Get lost!" shouted Witch Windbag and shut the door in her face. Poor Sid raced home. He passed Wotnot hunting for Leo who was already back on the rooftop.

Wonderwitch never found out how Wotnot and Windbag knew where she was. One minute, she was sitting on a chimney making cat brooches out of orange peel, and squeaking like a mouse. The next there was a rush of wind and they were clouting her with their broomsticks. Jet's owner came out to see what the noise was and hit them all with his golf club.

In the flurry of shouting and fighting, Wonderwitch caught her foot in the gutter and fell off the roof. Hanging upside down, three floors up, her money fluttering away into the trees, she did the only thing she could do.

She turned into a cat.

Bird Business

"Being a Wonderwitch, I could get on very well in business," the witch said, "but cats are so tricky." She was sitting on a chimney with six jelly babies in her mouth.

The cats were watching her. The black cat was talking to Fat Jack, Sweet Chebbs was washing saucer-eyed Flora, Sid, Leo and Jet were hiding and Poppet was stalking a green and yellow bird which was fluttering round an attic window.

"Birds," Wonderwitch said, "are no trouble at all. I love them. They don't eat a lot. They sing beautifully and they don't claw you to bits." The green and yellow bird hopped onto her hand. She popped it into her basket and jumped on her broomstick.

"I'm going into the bird business." She sailed round to Witch Wotnot who was polishing off a box of chocolates while she watched the television news.

"Hardly a bird of paradise," Witch Wotnot said. "It's a budgie."

The bird sang in a high clear voice. "Tweetie weetie! What a sweetie! I'll take it." trilled Wotnot, opening her purse. "I will only put it in a cage when I go out. I don't believe in cruelty."

The next night as Wonderwitch and the black cat landed on the rooftops, a boy's head poked out of the same attic window.

"Bogie!" he shouted, "Bogie . . . *Bogie.*" Then he saw the witch. "Have you seen a budgie, please?"

"No dear," she lied.

The boy kept on calling. He looked
everywhere. "Bogie's gone," he said sadly. "Do
you think I'll ever see him again?"

" . . . um, hum . . . I don't . . ." The black
cat dug his claws into the witch's leg and she
changed her mind, "I *do* think you will." Her
voice went into a scream, "I'll be looking
myself!"

"Thank you very much," he said. "My name
is Gregory, if you find him."

Of course Wonderwitch knew Witch Wotnot would never give Gregory's budgie back and she was too lazy to try and work out a spell to copy him. There wasn't another budgie like Bogie in the pet shop but there was a lovely parrot. She could steal that.

"If you're lucky," Wonderwitch told Wotnot, "sometimes these little budgies can suddenly turn into really big birds like parrots. Their feathers change colour overnight."

"Oh really!" Witch Wotnot answered rudely. "Since when did you know anything about birds?"

The parrot was magnificent and a good talker. While Witch Wotnot was out, Wonderwitch broke in and swopped him for the budgie.

That night she tapped on Gregory's bedroom window. When he woke up and opened it, she handed Bogie in.

"A good deed for a friend in need," she said to the black cat.

He choked.

Meanwhile Witch Wotnot, dressed in
green and yellow, was astonished. "Look, look!
My bird has grown. He's talking now and his
feathers are brilliant. I have a way with living
creatures."

She placed a titbit on her nose. "Mummy's
got a sweetie for her tweetie weetie."

The parrot pecked it off. "Give us a kiss
then."

Witch Wotnot couldn't stop boasting about her miracle bird. She was pictured in the local paper when she gave a lecture on birdcare. When Wonderwitch heard Witch Windbag was going to see the parrot, she slipped in secretly to teach him some new sayings.

Wotnot was dressed for Windbag's visit in so many colours she looked like a squashed flowerbed. "You see, my dear, birds adore me," she cooed to Windbag, swinging her pearls, "Oo's a littee bittee birdie then?"

"Don't mess with me, matie!" The parrot pecked the pearls and they bounced everywhere.

Windbag had hysterics.

She hurried round to see Wonderwitch. "I want one," she demanded jealously.

"Three thousand," said Wonderwitch.

"I'll wait," Windbag replied.

This time Wonderwitch decided to make a big effort with her magic. She shut herself up and started mixing and muttering. At one point she had twenty birds flying about the kitchen while she struggled to get it right.

Hours later, tired out, with Windbag bashing on the door, she made a silly mistake. She put two nines in the spell, an extra nought, and overdid the onion and essence of skunk. She turned into a bird herself.

A monstrous bird. Six feet tall. When she lumbered out of the kitchen with claws like huge spikes, eyes like golf balls and a beak like a split hatchet, Windbag screamed.

She was thrilled to bits.

As she took the bird home, Windbag couldn't stop laughing. "This Wonderbird is the biggest in the world," she said. "At least it will shut old Wotnot up."

It shut her up herself. The bird ate everything in the house and all the flowers and leaves in the garden. It splashed in the bath and water poured through the ceiling and down the stairs.

It had a nasty voice and talked all the time, ordering her about. "Dig up more worms, Windbag. Be quick or I'll peck you to pieces!"

Wonderwitch was having a fine time. She couldn't remember enjoying herself so much.

Windbag had stopped laughing long before she went to bed that night. Then she had nightmares. The bird danced like a herd of elephants and sang in a voice like a siren. When Windbag snored with her mouth open, Wonderbird plonked a foot in it.

In the next few days Witch Windbag lost weight with the worry while Wonderbird put it on. "I want my money back," Windbag said, "I don't want a bird at all."

But when she went to Wonderwitch's house, there was never anybody there. If the black cat knew anything, he wasn't telling.

Witch Windbag tried everything.

She stuck a 'FOR SALE' notice on the bird.

When it went out, she followed, in case it led her to Wonderwitch.

She was as desperate to get her three thousand pounds back as Wonderwitch was to keep it.

It was Wonderwitch who acted first. She was homesick. She left a note for Witch Windbag, signed with a mystery mark.

to whom it may concern
I'm writing you an honest word
to let you know i stole your bird.

She stuffed it under Windbag's teapot and skipped home, singing like a siren. She only stopped to eat up the flowers in Wotnot's garden.

When she had reached home and turned back into herself, she and the black cat went out for a ride on the broomstick.

Later, they had a celebration supper, and then Wonderwitch sat down to count her money.

It was gone!

In its hiding place under the sink she found a note.

TO WHOM IT MAY CONCERN

This reply is just to say

I took the cash and went my way.

School
Business

Wonderwitch was sitting on a chimney writing down her thoughts on being a Wonderwitch.

Ginger Sid, small black Jet and one-eyed Honeybun were asleep in a huddle. Old boy Bruiser was chasing saucer-eyed Flora and Poppet was feeding her kittens, born in a hidy-hole in the chimney wall.

Wonderwitch read aloud from her book. "Witches are liars, thieves, grumblers, greedy, clumsy, quarrelsome and *always* turning each other into toads. Why can't they be more like me? I could turn them into stars."

A wonderful idea was coming to her. "I'll go into the school business."

She bought a blackboard and desks and put an advertisement in *Witches Weekly*.

BE A STAR!

SHINE WHEREVER YOU ARE!

Wondercourse in Charm, Cookery & Culture

"I want to be a pop star," said Witch Windbag.

"I want to be a duchess," said Witch Wotnot.

"We want to shine," said Witch Woolly, Witch Wonky, Witch Weaselface, Witch Wellie and Witch Wormbody-Smith. Witches came from far and wide.

The Wondercourse started with a cookery class.

Wonderwitch greeted them in her tracksuit and chef's hat.

"Good morning ladies! Welcome!"

Nobody replied. Witch Wotnot was painting her nails with the parrot on her head, Windbag was singing, Wonky was eating a pizza with her feet on the desk. Weaselface and Woolly were having a quarrel. The noise was terrible.

"Quiet please!" Wonderwitch clapped her hands.

Nobody took any notice.

She wrote on the blackboard.

Rule 1: Shut up

The witches scowled.

Rule 2 SMILE

a star is always smiling

The witches stopped talking. *Smile?* Most of them didn't know how.

"Witch Wotnot," Wonderwitch pointed. "Would you be kind enough to give us a smile?"

Slowly Wotnot screwed up her nose, lifted her top lip and showed her teeth.

They all copied her.

"Very good!" Wonderwitch said, "You all look lovely! Now we can start our cookery lesson."

They were each making a cherry cake.

"Cream the butter and sugar," Wonderwitch explained, "then slowly beat in the eggs."

Witch Woolly, the clumsy one, knocked the flour bag onto the floor.

Windbag glared at Wonky. "You've stolen one of my eggs."

Wonky put her tongue out. "Drop dead!"

"Have my cake too!" Windbag shouted. She tipped the mixture over Wonky's head.

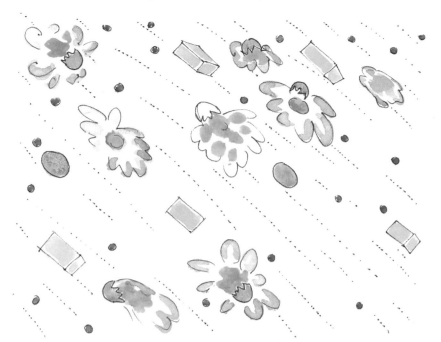

Wonky seized eggs. "Here's your egg, scum cake!" The eggs missed Windbag and hit Woolly.

Woolly hit Wotnot. Then a fight started. The air was filled with flour, eggs, cherries, butter.

"Ladies!" Wonderwitch swiped at the screaming witches' heads with her broomstick. "Duchesses never waste food!"

They all spent the rest of the day in bed, resting their black eyes, bruises and aching heads.

To be on the safe side, Wonderwitch took them outside next day. They played Grandmother's Footsteps to help them be less clumsy.

Wonderwitch was Grandmother. The others crept up behind to catch her. They turned into statues whenever she looked round to catch them moving.

The witches were clumsy. They made very funny statues. They bumped, knocked each other over, helped each other up and made friends again.

As time went on they grew quite fond of one another.

The course was really working.

In the daytime they learnt charm, cookery and culture. At night they had pillow fights and midnight feasts.

When Woolly dropped the Sunday dinner on Wonky's foot, Wonky only half turned her into a toad then turned her back. Wonky screwed up her nose and showed her teeth. They became best friends.

The course ended with a visit to a stately home.

Witch Wotnot travelled in the coach in a silver leotard, with rows of scarlet beads and flowers in her hair. "I hope to meet the duchess," she exclaimed. "It will change my life."

"Hear, hear!" echoed Windbag. "Stardom awaits!"

The day was a great success. The witches went round the house and saw the lions in the park. Everybody noticed them because they were arm in arm and smiling from ear to ear. One of them was singing pop songs.

While the others were buying postcards, Wotnot slipped through a door marked PRIVATE. She was helping herself to some hats when she met the duchess.

Luckily, the duchess was shortsighted. When she saw the silver leotard she thought it was the family ghost, and forgot about her hats.

The duchess was as
thrilled to meet the
witches as they
were to meet her.

"But do you turn
people into toads?"
she asked. "You seem
so cultured and
charming. Do you
really?"

Wonderwitch
explained they were
bored with that old trick.

"I wouldn't be bored with it," the duchess
answered. "Never, ever. I couldn't change
places with one of you, could I?"

The witches stared at her in astonishment.
She wanted to be a witch and they all wanted to
be duchesses.

"You do it," Windbag smiled at Wotnot.

"No, no . . . please," she replied, "it should be you."

They couldn't decide who the lucky witch should be. They were all so charming.

On the way home they stopped on the rooftops to see the cats. In the moonlight Poppet's grown-up kittens danced up to greet them. Nobody knew they were there so they hadn't got homes.

"Ohhhh . . ." sighed Witch Wotnot, cuddling a black fur ball who would warm her feet on cold nights, "I don't want to change places with anyone. This is all I want."

"Mmm . . ." agreed Witch Windbag, stroking a tabby head.

"Me too . . ." Witch Woolly popped a wriggling ginger bundle inside her jacket.

One by one the witches faded into the night taking the kittens with them. The older cats sat still, sniffing the air.

"I don't want to change places with anyone either." Wonderwitch put her arms round the black cat. "I like watching cats, watching each other. Being a Wonderwitch is the best thing in the world."

PRINTED IN BELGIUM BY

proost

INTERNATIONAL BOOK PRODUCTION